THE LEGEND OF YAOTL

by Steve Murphy

based on the screenplay by Kevin Munroe

illustrated by Patrick Spaziante

Simon Spotlight

New York   London   Toronto   Sydney

Based on the film *TMNT*™ by Imagi Animation Studios and Warner Bros.

SIMON SPOTLIGHT
An imprint of Simon & Schuster Children's Publishing Division
1230 Avenue of the Americas, New York, New York 10020
© 2007 Mirage Studios, Inc. *Teenage Mutant Ninja Turtles*™ and TMNT are trademarks of Mirage Studios, Inc.

Manufactured in the United States of America
First Edition
2 4 6 8 10 9 7 5 3 1
ISBN-13: 978-1-4169-4108-8
ISBN-10: 1-4169-4108-8

Nearly three thousand years ago an evil man opened an interplanetary portal in search of a magical power he'd read about in ancient books. But the power was too strong for him to control, and the portal set free creatures so dangerous and magic so dark that they almost destroyed Earth.

I am Observer Level-3.14. Eight thousand four hundred sixteen years ago, I was assigned to watch planet Earth. I was watching the night that the portal was opened, and I'm still carrying out my duty.

Strange things are happening on Earth, events dangerously similar to those that happened on that night thousands of years ago. It seems that in six days the same man will try to open the portal for the second time. To understand what this means, I must take you back in time to when the portal was first opened.

Long ago, before the ancient Mayan, Aztec, and Olmec civilizations existed, Central America was made up of separate states that together made up one nation, known as the Paxmec.

For thousands of years the Paxmec nation lived in peace and harmony. But then that peace came to an end. . . .

One day, about five thousand years into my observation, four South American warrior generals walked through the Paxmec world. Together they traveled through the land. They were evil and greedy. After they learned the magic of each civilization they came across, they destroyed it.

However these four warrior generals were not acting on their own orders. They were led by someone who was even more powerful and evil than they were. He was a mean and mysterious conqueror, and his name was Yaotl.

Within days Yaotl and his four generals destroyed the entire Paxmec nation. Then they traveled deeper into Central America until they found a new culture rich with magic, science, and technology. The civilization was called Xalica. It is considered the last great culture ever to be found on Earth.

Yaotl couldn't resist taking over this great civilization. He decided to call on this magical power from the portal to help him do so, to make sure its people knew to fear and obey him. The magical books told him to build a doorway for the portal, but that he had to wait for the Stars of Kikin to line up in order to activate it.

So he built the Shadow Gate from powerful stones, and then he waited. When he saw the stars aligning, he used all the dark magic he knew, and timed the army's attack with the opening of the portal.

Yaotl performed his dark spells of magic, and the Shadow Gate began to crackle. With a loud roar the sky parted and everything we knew about space and time changed. A portal to another world had been opened . . . and an army of monsters crossed the Shadow Gate down to Earth!

Yaotl thought he'd be able to control the monsters, to direct them against the Xalicans and force the people to surrender and obey him. But the monsters couldn't tell the difference between Yaotl, his generals, and the Xalicans. They were all the same in the eyes of the beasts, and the monsters attacked whomever crossed their path.

Yaotl had unknowingly destroyed the greatest culture man would ever know, and he had to be punished for this.

Sensing that something was wrong with her city, the most powerful Xalican shaman of all time, Siba-Noor, returned home from her journey to see the ruin that Yaotl had caused. In her anger she called on all of the magical powers to help her, and she cursed Yaotl and his four generals forever.

Siba-Noor turned the four generals into living stone. They were alive but unable to move and unable to die. They were trapped alone forever with the thoughts of the crimes they had carried out.

She cursed Yaotl with a never-ending life of pain,
forced to feel the loss of love over and over again.

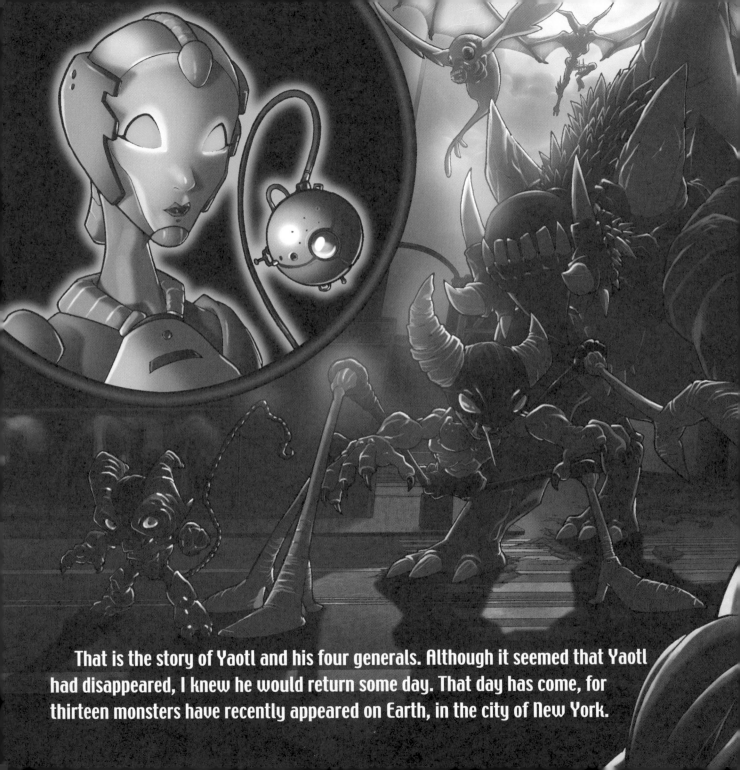

That is the story of Yaotl and his four generals. Although it seemed that Yaotl had disappeared, I knew he would return some day. That day has come, for thirteen monsters have recently appeared on Earth, in the city of New York.

These are the monsters I have spotted: Bigfoot, the Yeti, Lupa the werewolf, the slothlike Lethargo, the monkeylike Jersey Devil, the giant vampire bat Succubor, the llamalike Spitex, Vixx the fox, Azooli the puma, the wild boar Pict, the coati mundi Arkadin, the froglike Weeb, and the giant crocodile Cretaco.

They all seem to be drawn to a familiar dark energy . . . an energy that could only come from reuniting the four generals who were turned to stone: Aguila the eagle, Gato the jaguar, Serpiente the snake, and Mono, the ape without a tongue.

There can be only one explanation: The monsters and generals have been brought together by one man. He is the one who now holds onto the Shadow Gate. He is known to the people of Earth as the rich and mysterious Maximilian Winters. So what does this all mean?

The connection is clear: Yaotl is near, and in six days' time, when the Stars of Kikin align again, he will attempt to reopen the portal.

However I have also spotted four new creatures, mutant turtles with ninja powers, who seem to be working against Yaotl and his generals. What will happen is unknown, but from what I have seen, I have faith that these four turtles could be the ones to defeat Yaotl once and for all.

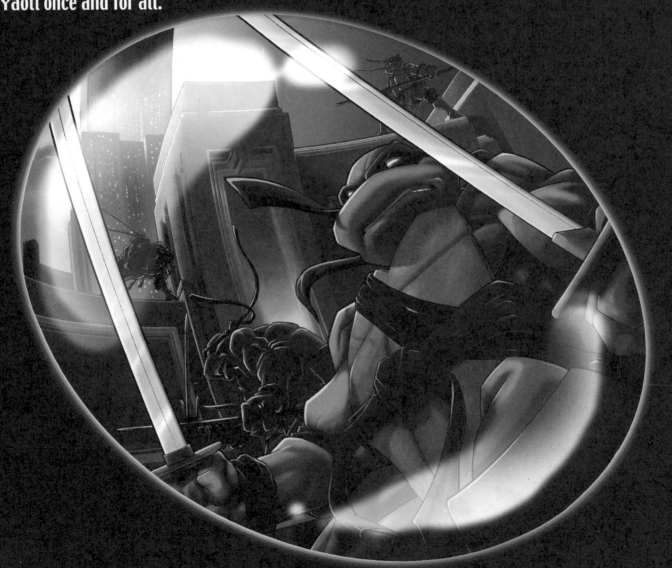